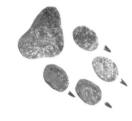

To Ella, Alice and Harriet, my fierce little chicks

and Jack, Ruth and Rebecca, the best friends a girl could have.

Love always, Kate x

Ω

Published by
PEACHTREE PUBLISHING COMPANY INC.
1700 Chattahoochee Avenue
Atlanta, Georgia 30318-2112
www.peachtree-online.com

Text and illustrations © 2019 by Kate Read

First published in the United Kingdom in 2019 by Two Hoots, an imprint of Pan Macmillan, a division of Macmillan Publishers International Limited.
First United States edition published in 2019 by Peachtree Publishing Company Inc.

The illustrations were created as mixed media with collage and painting.

Printed in March 2019 in China
10 9 8 7 6 5 4 3 2 1
First Edition

ISBN: 978-1-68263-131-7

Cataloging-in-Publication Data is available from the Library of Congress.

One Fox

A COUNTING BOOK THRILLER

Kate Read

PEACHTREE
ATLANTA

One
famished
fox

2

Two sly eyes

3

Three
plump
hens

four
padding
paws

5

Five
snug
eggs

6 Six silent steps

7 Seven knocks at the door

TAP!

TAP!

TAP!

8

Eight
beady
eyes

9 Nine flying feathers

10 Ten
sharp teeth

100 One hundred angry hens and . . .

. . . one frightened fox.

No hens or foxes were harmed in the making of this book.